MW00873607

# Colors

# of

# Chaos

By
**Carlo Kirk Polino**

**Copyright 2024**
**ISBN:** 9798322232506
**Imprint:** Independently published

# Prologue

Elementary school, we've all been through it. Pure fun with little to no rules or troubles. However, for some people, the best thing about it is the freedom to doodle. Just get your 24 pack of crayons and doodle your heart away! But once you reach middle school, that childhood joy disappears forever. Some people like growing out of this joyful phase and moving onto other mediums of art. Others want to stick with that joy until the very end of time. "You'll grow out of it too James, just like all of your friends have already, and when you do, you'll be a mature, big kid." James would have never listened to what his parents say, but this time, what if it was forced? But that's pretty much impossible and would never happen, right? Right.

# Chapter 1: A Crayony Good Start

James woke up from his snooze, "What a wonderful day it is!" He exclaimed while looking out the window. Just like all other mornings he turned on his favorite music to dance to, the **Razzmatazz Jig**. It was a Monday meaning school, so for most kids, this would be bad, horrible even! But for James, it's the best time of his life! He gets to hang out with his friends, Terry and Henry, have pizza for lunch, which always tastes amazing, but the best thing of all, doodle to no end. James was thinking about all this but suddenly, his parents called him. "James! Come downstairs! You don't want to miss school! Especially on your favorite day." His parents shouted.

"I'm coming!" James shouted while dancing, but before that, he had the big decision to make: what to wear. It determines how everyone thinks of you. Cool, funny, smart... you name it. But out of all the options James had, James picked out one of the best shirts he had, a crayon shirt. After all, he did love crayons to no end. The colors, the choices... they're amazing! And the perfect choice for the best day of the week! Now he had to get downstairs and hurry off to school.

His parents liked the outfit he chose but there was one slight problem about it. "James, crayons are for little kids, you should put on another, more mature shirt that doesn't have crayons." His parents told him. Surely, they wouldn't tell him to stop using crayons soon. That's one of the biggest parts of his life! James even has another shirt for that: "Sleep, Eat, Crayons, Repeat." Nonetheless, James picked out a generic art shirt. His parents liked it just the same. Now to deal with breakfast. James had the perfect breakfast meal: cereal with crayon marshmallows! He ate it extremely quickly, "The power of art fuels me!" He proclaimed, then off to school he went.

Because James lived relatively far away from school, he got to go on the bus. Before he left, his parents packed him something abysmal. When he opened his backpack, he saw a coloring book. which he would normally get every day on his bus ride to school, but to color the book... COLORED PENCILS! Unlike every other day where he got around 2 pages done, James didn't even finish ONE. Nonetheless, after a bus ride that literally circled around every area of his town, which is called Den Township, James arrived at school, where he met up with his friends, Henry and Terry.

Henry and Terry luckily were in the same classroom as James so they all could draw together when they had freetime. However, James still had to earn that freetime which could be very hard sometimes. Still, with the motivation to draw and have fun with his friends at the back of his mind, James breezed through even the toughest work at hand. Reading for James was a book club thing. He had to read up to chapter 4, and answer 3 questions for a book he was reading called **Vermillion Voyage**. James struggled with the questions a lot, mainly because it wasn't a picture book. Because James was already in 3rd grade, that meant no more picture books sadly.

He was able to push through the questions and he was then moved onto writing. During his freetime, he used what was available for crayons at school to draw. He then shifted to writing which was short, but boring.

James had to write a 100 word story with a partner. Luckily, he was partnered with his friend Terry. They titled the story, **The Dark Orange Dunes of Rueland**. They weren't very good with titles, but they made sure to include a color in there because of their shared love for drawing. Math was next up on the list of obstacles before being able to draw and it was tough, but at least the assignment let James color and draw, which was a huge plus. Because of the fact there was, well, drawing and coloring in it, James sped through it and quickly met up with his friends. Unfortunately, James discovered they had turned to the dark side. They both had colored pencils instead of crayons! James didn't comment on the fact they had turned on him, and just continued on with his day.

James had pizza for lunch which was served by the school cafeteria, and James absolutely loved it. He ate it way too fast that when he finished, there were still 10 minutes left until recess. James waited, and waited, and waited until those ten minutes were up. Recess was just playing on the swings with his friends. After recess, Social Studies was just pure boredom with it being just looking at the textbook for what felt like hours on end. Science was no better. It was just, BOB! BOB! BOB! BOB! It's always this science show called Bob Shy no matter what. At least this time it was about plants. From the moment on, when James heard a single color word, he watched it intently despite the fact that he has seen it so many times. Just from the focus on colors, he watched it, and surprisingly liked it too!

James' last stop for today was art. It was fun because it was crayon related art. The absolute best kind! But something struck him about the crayon container; it was missing some crayons! Only a couple, but with how much James loved crayons, he definitely noticed it and he was a bit annoyed about it. However, James could not do anything about it. Soon it was time to return home. He got onto the bus, took the unreasonably long trip back home, and arrived home on **Machesse Street**.

When he got there, James burst out of the bus and ran home as fast as he could. When he got inside, James asked his parents why they packed him colored pencils instead of crayons. They, for some reason, didn't tell him why. James soon after quickly finished his homework, mainly because it had drawing and coloring in it. After finishing it, he went to bed with quite a lot of thoughts in his head. "Why did my parents pack colored pencils instead of crayons? Why were there fewer crayons in art?" James fell asleep after forgetting about all these thoughts. Thus, the best day was now over, and the week would be downhill from here.

# Chapter 2: The Crayon Mystery

James woke up just like the day prior and turned on the **Razzmatazz Jig** just like he always did. However, something was definitely off. All of his crayon shirts were gone! Unlike yesterday where his parents just told him to not wear it, this time they straight up took it away! James was very annoyed about this, but carried on with his day anyway. "As long as I still have crayons, I'll be fine," he told himself. Now there was the question of what to wear. His parents always told him to not wear the same clothes two times in a row, so he picked out a tye dye shirt he made during summer camp. It was made with crayons surprisingly, and it was mostly yellow with a bit of orange here and there. He put it on along with a matching pair of pants he also made.

James went downstairs in a not so happy mood. He immediately went to his crayon box of 120, and for some reason, about half of the crayons were gone! He could've even lost the rarest color he had: Dandelion! But there was no time to search, only time to hurry up to school! He had breakfast, being his crayon cereal, of course, but unlike last time, the evilest thing was done. There weren't that many crayon marshmallows in the cereal! "Who could've done such a thing?! Whoever did this will pay!" he thought. Who would've done such a thing? His parents? Someone else who visited his house recently? James didn't know! He was just a young kid who absolutely loved crayons! These thoughts stuck like glue on his way to school.

Just like the day before, he didn't get a single page done on his coloring book. Even after the super long bus trip, he refused to use the colored pencils and got nothing done. Once again, he met with his friends outside of school but this time, James asked them about the fact that crayons were going missing. They didn't say anything, just like his parents did when he asked them about the colored pencils. "Surely school still has some crayons, I hope," James told himself as he went into class. School was just like the day before, with everything continuing from yesterday. For reading, James had to read the remainder of **Vermillion Voyage** and then answer questions related to the entire story. He somehow breezed through it unlike yesterday, mainly because he was worried that the crayons were taken away. Sadly, because of how much time he had left. James and his book club members had to choose a new book. They all chose something simple, **The Chartese Grasslands**. It was a lower level book but it was much easier and it was a picture book!

For writing, James and Terry continued work on **The**

**Dark Orange Dunes of Rueland**.
They breezed through it but their
teacher made them extend it to
200 words. They struggled a lot
with extending it, so much that
they couldn't even finish it by the
end of writing. Next was math. It
was so much harder than
yesterday. It was just plain
multiplication that James
struggled way too much on.
Luckily, because the smart kid
told the teacher to review the
homework, James didn't have to
worry about the lesson for at least
a little while. The homework on
the other hand, James aced!
The multiplication was super hard
since it was new to everyone. No
one understood it, James
struggled with it more than anyone
else. He didn't even finish it in
time for lunch! That meant he
couldn't check to see if any

crayons were missing. Next was lunch, where he could ask his friends if they noticed if there were any missing crayons. James asked them, but they did not say anything. James was surprised by this and simply continued to eat his lunch without talking with his friends at all. At least the sandwich his parents packed tasted pretty good. Recess was next up, and James chose to play on the playground instead of playing on the swings with his friends. He slid down the slide countless times, but then he saw something that caught his eye: Chalk.

James drew using his favorite color: bright green. He had a lot of fun just doodling away to his heart's content. It felt just like using crayons, which he hadn't used for a couple of days now. He drew mostly plants, and one alien on a small UFO in space. James then returned inside to, of course, the boredom that is Social Studies, but first, he had to get his homework for today. Dread, but not from the homework, Social Studies. James sat through the boredom and got to science somehow in one piece. Science was just as boring. It wasn't Bob Shy but instead something else that James felt so boring he forgot the name of it entirely! It was then time for specials. It was computers, with it being a free day to do whatever you want! James had so many questions, he searched up "crayons" on google and clicked a link to the main crayon company, **Crayart**. He looked for crayons there but there were no results for it. James almost cried because of this fact, but now it was time to go back home where he could tell his parents about everything. Before he left for the day, his teacher told the class something big... very big. "Tomorrow will be an off day and the day after that will be a field trip to **Crayart**!"

After the long bus ride home, he rushed to the door and asked his parents "Where did all the crayons go?! I looked on **Crayart's** own website but there was nothing!" James exclaimed. His parents then finally told him the truth.

"**Crayart** got rid of crayons because the owner says crayons are for babies," his parents told him.

"Well, why do you seem to be getting rid of all my crayons?!" James shouted. His parents didn't reply back. James went to bed with plans, big ones. He would bring back crayons for all kids! For now, though, he could only dream.

# Chapter 3: The Caribbean Green Crayon Team

James woke up just like the days prior, but he was not happy at all. All crayons were probably gone from his 120 box and they were never coming back. Nonetheless, he turned on the **Razzmatazz Jig** and put on his clothes. He rushed downstairs, not because he had school, but to look for his crayons. James didn't see anything in his crayon box, except for one crayon: Caribbean Green. James decided he would incorporate the crayon into his plan, and thus, the **Caribbean Green Crayon Team** was formed. Before he could do anything, James had to have his breakfast. It was extremely disappointing. When James peeked into the box, all the crayon marshmallows were gone. James didn't even want to eat until he got answers for all of this. This time he would get all the answers he needed.

James finally asked his parents about everything. "Mom, Dad, why have all my crayons and crayon marshmallows and everything related to crayons have been disappearing?!" At last, his Mom replied with the truth.

"It turns out, son, every crayon and crayon related thing is owned by **Crayart**. Every shirt, cereal, and even other crayon brands are all owned by **Crayart**."

His Father then continued, "We had to give everything back to **Crayart** at a huge recall event they had."

"James, we are so sorry about everything," his mom added. "Even if we can't do anything about the recall, we will do whatever we can to help you with your situation." James then told his parents about his plan.

"I also have something to say. I started plans for what I call the **Caribbean Green Crayon Team**. Maybe you two can help me spread the word?"

His parents then happily told him, "We'll do everything we can to help you."

James finally had some hope for the future. His parents, now onboard with his plan, would not listen to **Crayart** and not bring back the Caribbean Green crayon.

James' first step for his plan was an advertisement poster. They drove to their local dollar store, known as Dollar Duckie, to get some supplies. It took a little while to get to Dollar Duckie but once they got there, in place of any crayons, there were none other than colored pencils and lame markers. James quickly picked out a nice sky blue poster for the **Caribbean Green Crayon Team**. They then drove back home, but not before telling the cashier about the **Caribbean Green Crayon Team**.

James worked tirelessly on the poster, but with only one color, it was pretty hard to draw anything. He finished the poster by around 3pm, the time where he would usually leave school, but there was no time for thoughts! There was only time to spread the word around! His parents made a form before they left for people to sign-up and join the team and save all the crayons!

They all went to downtown Den Township to recruit members for the **Caribbean Green Crayon Team**. James and his family first went to the park and by pure coincidence, they found Terry and Henry playing on the swings! James immediately joined in and told them about the **Caribbean Green Crayon Team**, which James abbreviated as **CGCT**. "Hello good friends!" James exclaimed.

"Hi there." They both muttered.

"I have plans for something I like to call the **Caribbean Green Crayon Team** or **CGCT**!" James told them excitedly.

"Ugh, don't get us started on

crayons." Terry said.

"Wait, Terry, do you even remember seeing any crayons recently?" Henry asked.

"Hmm, no times that I remember." Terry said.

"That's exactly why I started **CGCT**! **Crayart** got rid of any and all crayons!" James told them.

"What about off brands?" Terry asked.

"They're actually owned by **Crayart** along with anything else crayon related!" James exclaimed.

"Then I guess we will join you!" His friends both stated.

"Well you can! Just have your parents fill out this form to join the **Caribbean Green Crayon Team**!" James explained as their parents began to quickly fill out the form.

James and his family continued driving around town

recruiting a lot of people to **CGCT**. Most of the people who ended up joining had kids who loved crayons so much that they convinced their parents to join. They went to bakeries, other playgrounds, and pretty much everywhere in Den Township with people in it. They even went into some huge stores and got a manager of an entire store to join! But by the end of the day, they could only recruit a grand total of 94 people to the **Caribbean Green Crayon Team**.

The sun was setting and with only 94 people, James knew that it wouldn't be enough to bring all crayons back! Billboards seemed like the best option to gain more members, but how could they get it in time?! Luckily, by pure coincidence, one of the members of **CGCT**, Sally, actually could make the billboard in time. Sally was a pretty well-known billboard maker in Den Township, and even places beyond it. One of the parts of the form was to put your phone number, so James' Mom was able to call her. "Hi, is this Sally?" James' Mom asked.

"Yes, it is! How can I help you?" Sally asked.

"You know how there was that whole thing, that **Caribbean Green Crayon Team**?" His Mom asked.

"Yeah! Of course I remember that! I'm a part of it!" Sally exclaimed.

"Perfect! We need a billboard fast!" His Mom then quickly explained what they wanted the billboard to say. Sally was happy to help.

"I'll get straight to it, bye!" Sally said as the call ended.

James then ate dinner, pizza specifically, and then he was off to bed. Before he went to bed, his parents told him something big. It turned out, the trip to the **Crayart** factory would be way too long for a single bus drive, so they had to stay at a hotel nearby. James' parents told him they would actually be coming, too, and they could all discuss everything about the **Caribbean Green Crayon Team**. With all this happening by tomorrow, James was able to rest happily.

# Chapter 4: The Big Day

It was time… it was finally time for the field trip. James woke up with pure determination to revive all crayons. He almost instantly turned on the **Razzmatazz Jig** just like every other day before, but unlike all other days he went extremely fast! James got dressed in a matter of seconds! He chose to put on one of his least worn shirts that sat in the back of his drawer saying "Do you think I look Bluetiful today?" He added a matching pair of Bluetiful pants to go with it. James then ran downstairs, not because of time or crayons, but to discuss some things with his parents before the trip.

"Perfect timing son!" His

Mom said.

"We have something big to share about **CGCT**!" His Dad then exclaimed.

"What is it?" James asked.

"The billboards did great and are all over the place!" His Mom told him.

"We also made a form website to recruit even more people!" His Dad added.

"Did anyone else have any crayons?" James asked.

"As a matter of fact, some kids did have crayons! We even have a website page for anyone to show their crayons!" His Dad explained.

James after talking had only 10 minutes left. So, just like the days prior, he ate cereal, but it was different. James' parents bought one of the few remaining crayon cereal with a whole bunch of crayon marshmallows in there! He ate it incredibly quickly. Before he was about to go, he told his parents about the coloring book and that he made no progress in it because he wouldn't use colored pencils. Luckily, some people donated some crayons for James to use. He put all the crayons into a small 8 pack he had and then went onto the bus for school.

During the bus ride, James was able to color a total of 5 pages! James also saw something shocking: billboards everywhere he looked! Another, and another, and another! All for the **Caribbean Green Crayon Team**! He got to school and everyone was talking about **CGCT**. James chose to politely ignore it and went into class. James only had around 10 minutes of free time before the trip began so he used this on the coloring book. One page after another, in total finishing another 3 pages, but then it was finally time to go. James already used the bathroom at home meaning he wouldn't need to use it again. Onto the bus his class and all of the third grade went. It was boring, very, very boring. His teacher said that it would take at least 6 hours to get there! But as his parents told him, there would be a hotel they would go to when they arrived.

After an incredibly long road trip. James and all of 3rd grade finally got to the hotel. During this half of the trip, James got 12 pages of his coloring book done and he saw 3 billboards for **CGCT**! James got to the room he was assigned after maneuvering through the hotel with some of the staff. He then finally met up with his parents who were waiting there.

"James! You're finally here!" They both exclaimed.

"I was able to finish 17 pages of my coloring book!" James told them.

"We have something big to say too!" His Mom said.

"Using the website, over 20,000 people joined the **Caribbean Green Crayon Team**!" His Dad informed him.

"Something else related to that, I saw 3 billboards on my way here!" James said.

"That's great!" They both answered. James and his family then ate some food at the hotel. Because the bus trip was so long, they stayed at the hotel for the entire day along with everyone else who came with them.

James spent most of his

time drawing with every crayon he had as the members of **CGCT** grew. The total went from 20,000 up to 30,000, all the way up to 50,000 members! Because it was 3pm, the time where most people would be heading back from work, more and more people were seeing the billboards. James then had a snack that his parents packed earlier in the day. Then he continued drawing and coloring his coloring book until dinner. James sat down with his friends Henry and Terry and shared some crayons with them. They also showed James some of their remaining crayons. Suddenly, out of nowhere, the idea clicked on how to win against the owner of **Crayart**: a drawing battle. He told this to his family right before he went to bed and they thought it was a good idea. James slept, with dreams of the grand return for all crayons.

James got up, and was ready for the other half of the trip. He was glad his parents would come with him since this half of the trip was actually 4 hours long! James didn't even need the **Razzmatazz Jig** to get up and moving; he was just that determined. James ate breakfast which was just normal cereal but he didn't even care a bit! He got dressed in an instant, too, and then was off with the rest of his family! James got on the bus with his parents and left the hotel. The trip went pretty slow as he and his family approached the long awaited **Crayart** headquarters. James finished another 19 pages of his coloring book and saw 5 billboards in total along the way. His parents, before getting off the bus, told him that the number of people in **CGCT** was now 200,000! When James heard that, he felt they actually had a chance with this! They then walked into the gates of no return, the **Crayart** headquarters. In that moment, James felt the most anxious he ever felt in his entire life.

# Chapter 5: The CEO Standoff

James entered the gates with his family and friends after some hesitation. James was both anxious and excited at the same time. His new updated plan was to do a drawing battle against the literal owner of **Crayart** and with everyone being a member of the **Caribbean Green Crayon Team**, they would say James' art is better. James then told his plan to his friends and family before going in.

"I have a plan!" James said.

"What is it James?" Henry asked.

"A drawing battle against the owner of **Crayart**!" James exclaimed.

"How in the world would you win?" James' Mom asked.

"With so many people being a part of the **Caribbean Green Crayon Team**, they would all say my art is better! We just need to be sure they can vote on the contest" James explained.

"We're all in!" Everyone exclaimed. James' Dad began work on an updated website for the drawing battle with a new poll page to vote on.

They went into the **Crayart** factory soon after. James was excited but also worried about going up against the actual CEO of **Crayart**. He was glad his family would be there to support him.

The first stop on the trip was to the **Crayart** store. Where James and everyone else discovered something none of them knew about. Apparently, **Crayart** had held "The Battle of Crayons and Colored Pencils!" that culminated in a final drawing battle just like in James' plan! But unlike his plan, the crayons lost and were pulled from every store in existence. In place of all crayons, there were colored pencils, not even markers for a short time! This made James far more determined than ever. The next stops were how colored pencils and markers were made. For markers, they had a marker maker on display and behind it, there was the actual, bigger way they made markers. Henry got distracted by the marker maker and the big machine that made the markers in bulk.

The remainder of the group continued onto the section showcasing how colored pencils were made. It pretty much showed the main lead of the pencil being dipped in some kind of dye and then put inside the pencil. Terry was even more mesmerized by the dipping process. "Pick up then dip, pick up then dip." He repeated to himself. The last stop was the shutdown crayon factory, which the employees told the group not to go through. The tour was completed after that, but they still were unable to confront the CEO! James and his family had no other choice but to leave and go back to the hotel. As they were about to leave, James and his family realized something big: CGCT now had a total of 1 million members. They also noticed something was off with the **Crayart** logo. It was completely grayscale except for one stripe, Caribbean Green, Just as James noticed that, it was too late. The bus began to drive out of the parking lot spot it was in which was labeled as number 29, Purpvilo. Everyone then returned back to the hotel after another long drive. This time, James saw a total of 14 billboards and finished 13 pages of his coloring book!

Everyone had to pour back out of the bus despite no one wanting to. Because of how big **CGCT** got, everyone wanted to go back to **Crayart** and bring back the crayons. Unsurprisingly, they had to go back to the hotel or else everyone would be far too tired. James was pretty annoyed, but at the same time very relieved. Just imagine how long it would take to make another trip back and forth! He had dinner with his family and friends and then went to bed once more.

The next morning it was finally time to go back and save the crayons. James woke up, quickly got dressed, ate breakfast, and with everyone else, got on the bus to save all crayons! James and everyone else got back to the **Crayart** HQ after another very long drive with far too many billboards. With no hesitation, they went in and breezed through everything on display. Terry spotted a staircase that seemed like it would get everyone to the CEO's room. James' Dad had already finished the poll so now all that was left to add were the images to vote upon. After getting to the CEO's room, their showdown could now begin.

"Well, well, well, look who we have here, the **Caribbean**

**Green Crayon Team**, hah! What a stupid name." The CEO exclaimed when everyone reached his office.

"We're here to bring back crayons no matter what!" James shouted.

"We'll see about that. You don't even have any crayons!" The CEO exclaimed.

"Don't say that in front of my friend!" Shouted Henry.

"Besides, we have our own!" Terry exclaimed. Suddenly, a whole crowd of random CGCT members flooded through the newly opened entrance as if they were summoned into the CEO's room, with each person having their own crayons they then gave to James.

"Why in the world are you all here!?" The CEO shouted.

"To save crayons once and for all!" The crowd exclaimed.

44

Immediately, the crowd left, leaving only a huge pile of crayons behind. James' friends and his family collected all the crayons and gave them to James. "How about this, **Crayart** owner! We do a drawing contest, and if I win, all crayons will return!" James shouted.

"I accept the deal, but if I win, only colored pencils forever!" The CEO shouted as they shook hands. James' Mom passed out two pieces of paper that the CEO had and James' Dad started a 15-minute timer. They settled on the theme, "outer space". And thus, they began the contest.

James began in a hurry, going super-fast but calmed down knowing he's pretty much guaranteed to win. The CEO on the other hand, was doing super well and taking his time. James was worried after seeing the CEO in such a lead, but then he remembered he would still win in terms of colors! He added as much color as physically possible to the point where it looked professional for a 3rd grader. Finally, time was up, and the images were uploaded to the poll so everyone could vote. James' drawing was of a lavender planet with rings and a little alien city on top. The CEO's drawing was of an astronaut in space, very simple, but very high quality. Nearly instantly, a vote came in, then another, and then some more, until there were more than 1 million votes. With a 98% majority, James won.

"How in the world did a child win against me?!" The CEO shouted. "I demand a rematch!" James reluctantly agreed. Once again, James' Mom passed out paper, and his Dad set a timer, this time, it was only for 5 minutes and the theme was "garden".

Both the CEO and James were vigorous with their drawing. James drew a standard garden with a tree, while the CEO drew a field of flowers instead. Once again when the voting was completed, the CEO lost, partly because the poll was slightly rigged, and mostly because the CEO was only half-done coloring. "Ok Fine! You win, I'll bring back all the crayons." The CEO promised. Everyone was thrilled with the news that all crayons would finally return. But first, everyone had to get back to Den Township.

# Chapter 6: The Return Home

The drive back home felt the most refreshing out of all the trips back and forth to the hotel. James was able to finally finish up his coloring book after getting to the hotel for the last time. Everyone was able to quickly get back into their rooms including James and his family.

"Great job James!" His Mom said.

"Thanks for everything. I really couldn't have done it without all of you." James exclaimed.

"I got you another coloring book!" His Dad told him. "I knew the day would come where you would need a new one!"

"Perfect!" James exclaimed. Finally, it was time for the last dinner before they had to return to Den Township. Henry and Terry were there.

"Amazing job back there James!" They both said.

"You really showed that CEO who's boss!" Henry exclaimed.

"It was my parents who helped the most by making the poll on the website." James explained.

"Still, you stood for what was right." Terry answered.

"And the art looked very good!" Henry complimented. James and his family finished their dinner, and then they all went to bed. That night James' dreams were amazing, He felt like a hero.

James woke up for the final trip back home. He got ready, but this time, with the **Razzmatazz Jig** back on. James found one crayon related shirt that his parents brought and James wore it. It said, "I'm colorful, and brave," with a superhero crayon on it. Very fitting for what James just went through. His breakfast was the remainder of the other non-crayony cereal. Then they were finally off to Den Township.

Before returning home, the hotel gave them three special things: a small crayon minifigure that **Crayart** gave to James, a small pack of crayons that the hotel had, and lastly, one special crayon called Jamered. It was similar to brick red, but a bit more orange. The trip back was relatively quick since it was the shorter half of the trip. James was able to finish a total of 7 pages of his new coloring book, but unlike every other time, he saw no billboards for the **Caribbean Green Crayon Team**. The billboards seemed to have disappeared right after the big deciding poll was posted on the website. Finally, James got home after the long, long, bus ride.

As soon as James was home, he instantly fell onto the couch, and then fell asleep for a total of 4 hours! When James woke up from his snooze, he chose to draw, just like he always did. He drew, and colored, and even made some comics while he was at it! He used the pack of crayons he got from the hotel as a gift for saving all crayons. The doodling made him really appreciate being a kid, but at the same time, he had been mature enough to stand up for what was right and bring back all crayons. Drawing got boring after a while so he resorted to TV. His parents were also watching something, but it was not what James expected. It was of him and his family! They all somehow were on the global news for saving crayons! The news person then mentioned the **Caribbean Green Crayon Team** and began listing some of the most important members that even James didn't know about! At that moment, James actually cried because he was so overwhelmed with emotion. His parents did their best to comfort him, but they instead joined in with him. They had been able to make a huge difference by saving all crayons in the world.

Soon after, his thoughts finally settled as it was time for dinner. James really didn't want to talk about what they just accomplished, as most of dinner was silent with the **Razzmatazz Jig** playing in the background quietly. James had grilled cheese, which was very rare to have for dinner. When dinner was over, James pretty much went straight to bed with no questions asked. Finally the dust had truly settled, and James could finally rest happy.

# Chapter 7: The Return to Crayony Normalcy

James woke up after the best rest of his entire life. Finally, he was home at last, and since it was a Sunday, that meant no school! The only bad thing was that it meant James couldn't discuss what happened to his class! James, just like all other days, turned on the **Razzmatazz Jig**, got dressed, then ate his precious crayon cereal. It somehow tasted better than any other time he had eaten it! The first thing James wanted to do after his morning routine was to get some more crayons for a new project he was planning. Currently in his box of 120 crayons, there were no neon crayons or special effect crayons. There weren't too many regular crayons yet, mainly because **Crayart** still hadn't returned all of the crayons. Even the crayons other people gave to him weren't an option because his parents gave them all back. At least he had the pack of 16 the hotel gave him, and the Jamered crayon he got, too. Nonetheless, James had to go to his nearest Dollar Duckie to reobtain some of his crayons, and get some new special effect crayons in the process.

James told his parents about his plans and they happily drove him to Dollar Duckie. The trip was

much, much faster than anything
James had ever experienced,
mainly because the last few trips
he was on were incredibly long in
comparison. James and his family
soon arrived to a shocker; there
were crayons everywhere! It
seemed that what James did has
caused **Crayart** to have a huge
crayon sale and have stores fill
aisles with crayons! There were
crayons pretty much everywhere,
even in aisles crayons aren't
supposed to be in! It was way too
unusual to pass up. And of course,
well, crayons. It was pretty easy
for James to pick out the crayons
he needed: neon crayons,
construction paper crayons, and
more! He picked out a piece of
poster paper to use as his poster.
Pretty soon, it was time to head
home. James and his family put
every crayon and the poster into

their car, and then they all returned home.

What James was planning was a poster about what he just went through with **Crayart** that he would share with his entire class, because no one other than his friends and family knew what happened there. Of course, he would use Caribbean Green for most of the poster, the heart and soul of the **Caribbean Green Crayon Team**. Then he used some of the crayons he had to recreate the drawing he made at the CEO's HQ. James worked tirelessly on the poster all afternoon. He drew about the whole adventure, wrote about the experience of it, and colored the whole thing, and with some time, and a lot of dedication, he was able to finally finish the entire poster.

The next day he would present the poster and talk about what he went through. By the time he finished, it was already dinner time and James could finally show his poster he worked on all afternoon!

"Mom, Dad, I finally finished my poster!" James exclaimed as he showed the poster to his parents.

"It looks great!" His Mom complimented.

"I worked really hard on it and I want to present it to my class tomorrow!" James told them. James and his family then ate dinner like normal after that.

After dinner, James carefully rolled up his poster and put it into his backpack. Then it was finally bedtime for James. It was very easy for him to fall asleep because of all that had happened

during the field trip, making him
very tired. James rested happily.

# Chapter 8: The Story's End

James finally woke up a while after his alarm went off. With how well he slept, it was very hard for him to get up and moving. James turned on the **Razzmatazz Jig** just as he always did and he began to do his morning routine. In his drawer, his parents were able to get back the crayon shirt he had wanted to wear last Monday. Of course, he chose it, and then quickly ran downstairs. He ate the last bit of his crayon cereal that he had remaining and was soon ready to go. He got on the bus, and went off to school. James colored 2 pages with his new 16 pack he got from the hotel during the field trip. He arrived at school but unlike last time, the trip there didn't feel that long. Nonetheless, he met up with Henry and Terry just like he always did and then went to class. For reading, James and his book club members were somehow able to finish **The Chartreuse Grasslands** pretty quickly, mainly because it was a picture book unlike **Vermillion Voyage**. But with that easiness, they had to answer a total of 15 questions about it! It was hard, mainly because of how many days 3rd grade had been off from school, and because of that, every 3rd grader struggled a lot with pretty much every school thing they had to do that day. James struggled with the questions a lot just like everyone else in his book club, but somehow, he was able to finish all 15 questions before reading was over. James, wanting to present his poster, asked his teacher when he could show it off. His teacher said he could present it as soon as reading was over. James then waited, and waited for what felt like forever until reading was finished. He then finally could present it.

The class was amazed with it. It was very detailed, and even the teacher liked it a lot, mainly because it used both art and writing amazingly well! The teacher decided to hang it up on the wall for everyone to use as inspiration for any writing they had to do.

The next class was writing which James and Terry were able to breeze through. They were finally able to finish **The Dark Orange Dunes of Rueland** and once again, the teacher was very impressed by it. So much so that the teacher even let them present their story first! Math was very easy since it was another coloring thing. Lunch was mostly talk about what James did, and literally everyone was talking about it. The principal actually had to come into the cafeteria and shush everyone. Recess was mostly swinging with Henry and Terry until it was over. Social Studies was even more textbook boredom, but at least James could kinda focus on it, but only sort of. Science was well, science, meaning even more Bob Shy and even more boring worksheets! Finally, came computers. It was just typing practice like usual, boring, but at least James was able to get his typing speed up to 15 words per minute. Finally, James was dismissed from school.

The bus ride home once again went by super-fast. James finished 1 page this time. Finally, he got home onto **Macheese Street**. James ran right home and met up with his parents.

"How was school?" His Dad asked.

"Great for the first day back after a long time!" James exclaimed.

"We have a big surprise for you!" His Mom said.

"What is it?" James asked.

"Come inside and you'll see!" His Momtold him. James went inside and he saw the biggest crayon ever! And it was his color, Jamered, too!

"I love it!" James exclaimed. He immediately drew something with it but it was pretty hard to use. James drew a big crayon with a heart around it. "Give this to **Crayart**." He told his parents. His Mom then went to the mailbox and dropped it off.

"How was your presentation?" His Dad then asked.

"It went great!" James exclaimed.

James then drew for quite a while, even missing his snack! He had fun just drawing with Jamered and other colors. Soon it was finally time for dinner. He had spaghetti and meatballs, one of his favorites for dinner. Then, it was time for bed just like every day, but this one was the most colorful snooze of them all.

# Epilogue

About a day after James finished his letter, it arrived at the Crayart HQ. The staff saw it and it was given straight to the CEO, of course, and the CEO loved it. So much that the CEO decided to write a letter back.

"Dear, James. After you beat me, I decided to give crayons a try for once. One of my employees actually had a coloring book that they offered to me, and luckily in my office, there was one leftover crayon that I could use. I chose to just do one page and I expected nothing from it, but I soon found it really fun! I really do apologize for getting rid of crayons, I was being far too irrational. Thank you for inspiring me. The CEO."

After another day, the CEO's letter got back to James. James loved the entire thing. And thus, the CEO had finally made up his mind, and crayons were back for good, never to disappear again.

# The
# End

# Author's Note

I hope you enjoyed this book! This is the first book I have ever written in my entire life! There is one final thing! Have you found all of the color words scattered around the book? Here are two hints for them!

1: Some are crayon names!
2: As the book progresses, the colors go in rainbow order!

# Thank You for Reading Colors of Chaos.

# About the Author

**Carlo Kirk Polino** is an 11-year-old fifth grader. *Colors of Chaos* is his first book. Carlo enjoys studying math and science, as well as playing and coding video games. Of course, he also loves art and is a big fan of crayons.

Carlo lives in Point Pleasant, New Jersey with his parents and sister, Sofia.

Made in United States
North Haven, CT
15 April 2024

51358464R10043